CRADLELAND
OF PARASITES

BY SARA TANTLINGER

Published by Strangehouse Books
an imprint of Rooster Republic Press LLC
www.rooosterrepublicpress.com
roosterrepublicpress@gmail.com

"Bubonic Litany" was originally published by Dissections
Horror E-Zine in 2018.

ISBN:
978-1-946335-36-4

Find our catalog at
www.roosterrepublicpress.com

TABLE OF CONTENTS

"We see death coming into our midst like black smoke, a plague which cuts off the young, and a rootless phantom which has no mercy for fair countenance. Woe is me of the shilling in the armpit; it is seething, terrible, wherever it may come, and a head that gives pain and causes a loud cry, a burden carried under the arms, a painful angry knob, and a white lump. It is of the form of an apple, like the head of an onion, a small boil that spares no one. Great is its seething, like a burning cinder, a grievous thing of an ashy colour. It is an ugly eruption that comes with unseemly haste. They are similar to the seeds of the black peas, broke in fragments of brittle sea-coal and crowds precede the end. It is a grievous ornament that breaks out in a rash."

- Welsh poet Jeuan Gethin, 1349, on the arrival of the plague.

On a White Horse

I am the rider of the white horse
enigmatic in interpretation

I do not ride as the Holy Spirit,
you will find no gospel spread
beneath my horse's hooves

I do not ride as prosperity
nor as war, but you could find
both, if summoned correctly

In the name of Pestilence, I ride,
your sacred lord of contagion
bow down beneath divine damnation

As my horse gallops on, I draw back
my bow, a bleeding sun overhead
turns sky to crimson as my brass
quiver demands death; arrows
poisoned with disease fly through
the world, spreading epidemics
abroad in devastating silence

Noble demise in hallowed ground
beckons, come to my earthen embrace
sleep forever in bodily betrayal
as organs shut down, as blood runs
infected and uncured -- follow white
mane and tail through the darkness
to me, your blessed liberator gifting
kernels of bacteria to burrow inside skin

In the name of Pestilence, I ride

PLAGUE OF ATHENS

My palm against your forehead
detects violent heat, unrelenting
with its fiery grip on your brain

You blink at me with inflamed eyes,
puffy redness like clouds of dragon fire
burning through retinas as blood rages
in your throat, on your tongue, fetid
breath assaults my senses as sieges
and war continue for the second year

The retching, the coughing, haunts all
soldiers, your convulsions scaring
them off as if merely glancing at you
would transmit sickness onto them,
but I stay, defeated on all fronts
knowing your heat will consume us all,
morphing skin to blotches of pustules

You mumble of thirst despite the water
I pour down your desert throat, no liquid
satiates what burns inside those bones;
fever strikes men at war, so intense
in its vehement fervor that they strip armor,
run mutilated and naked through battlefields
seeking cold ponds to dunk feverish bodies in,
maybe to drown away both disease and battle

Birds arrive, dropping low to feast
on carcasses, but even they only peck
once before cawing and spiraling far
away from this place of sickness,
the vulture who stays and eats, who
devours spoiled rot, cannot process
carrion such as this, and I watch

as even the underworld birds pale and die

What is the cause of our affliction?
What has struck my fellows down
to nothing more than sacks of flesh
too weak to fight, to breathe?
I will wonder about toxins in the wells,
polluted grain, or is it dark power
sent to cleanse us from the earth?
Have the oracles in Sparta found
a way to end our existence at last?

Beneath the God of Plague we suffer,
human law no longer a threat that matters
as fear of death runs rampant between
horrendous crime, citizens spending
money foolishly, refusing to obey codes,
discarding honor, all too afraid of the death
sentence disease has wrought within town

I abandon your corpse and the soldiers'
bodies, I abandon war and Spartan threat
as even enemies refuse to come closer,
I walk through tides of misbehavior
people doubting religion as even temples
transform into places of great misery

and wherever I walk, plague follows,
silently waiting beneath boot steps
beckoning me onward to spread its gift
residing on my fingertips, in my spit,
inviting as much of the population as
I can to join me in these final days,
hoping that painful but quick death
will be better than what we leave behind,
will be better than the aftermath of Athens.

THE DEMON OF CONSTANTINOPLE

Malevolent spirit who appears in night terrors
hovering over sleeping bodies, casting curses;
when the dreamers wake, they'll find heated heads
simmering with fever, pestilence sweeping
through the Roman Empire without mercy
and nor will ruler Justinian grant clemency
when collecting tax from the sick, from
deceased neighbors; there is no pity
in times of terror, no charity to be granted

Bar the doors, let no one inside, even family
members forbidden to visit, yet when they sleep
and dream, he comes, the demon dripping
blood like boiled shadows, invoked by traitors
seeking a god of health, but summoning only
he who rains arrows of plague down unto people
mincing hope to nothing but scraps of bloody panic

The plague must be appeased before it is removed,
this demon will kill by the hundreds, thousands,
millions if he must -- anything to satisfy the great
thundering hunger in his empty belly for fear,

to crunch on bones drenched in mucus and terror,
to delight in the screaming of dreamers unable to wake
urges the demon to feast and feast, no invocation,
no exorcism will cast him away until he is satisfied,
until the number of dead stacked outside in the open,
nowhere to bury them, sends deafening laughter
rippling throughout his coppery veins, only then
will these darkest days of punishment be lifted

The Justinian Plague

Is this annihilation?
I have no choice
but to think Heaven
tired of moral vice,
sent down a scourge
to banish the planet
of us, its greatest violator

I have seen their swellings,
melon-sized and dark
as rotten fruit, oozing
liquid stenches worse
than falling face-first
into a pile of dung

Uncle grew black blisters,
fell into a sleep he never
awoke from, then died,
father spiraled into delusion
sprouted paranoia
and stuffed his mouth
with hemlock

Bodies dumped into the ocean
keep washing back up, bloated
with sea water and fish,
bobbing on the shore like ghosts
too tired to finish their haunting

When the monks come, we run,
they will try to exorcise
anyone in contact with corpses
as if we chose to suffer
among rotting bodies

For all I know, the monks
carry such pestilence
spread it throughout towns
on purpose, are nothing
but messengers of ruin,
creating excuses for power

Is this annihilation?
I have no choice
but to follow my family
into the depths of death
where cool earth invites
underground slumber
as the last option for hope

HER FACE OF BONE NEEDLES

Down her back, they fall
viruses disguised as smooth snakes
glittering with obsidian scales
welcoming darkness's dominion
over all that will curse this world

From hair follicles, they sprout
forgotten spores morphed
into slithering pythons,
she is no Medusa, no saint
or goddess, something greater --
this demon named Plague

Forward she glides, phantom-like,
a memory reborn during panicked chaos
seeking attention, seeking you
wondering how your blood tastes
as she commands you, her host cell,
dissolving through lipids like acid

Plague hungers for a full embrace,
her genetic instructions envelope
atoms intent on destruction as she
brings you closer into her bosom
while needles sprout from her face

Sharp pinprick branches tattooing bloody
images through your skin, onto your bones,
carving out a remedy that you cannot see,
will never discover, can only claw open
your own flesh in desperate hope to discover
directives left behind by Plague's wrath

Too late, too late --
her face of bone needles consumes

you whole and raw, crushing white
blood cells and antibodies into dust;
you will return to the beginning,
to oxygen and iron, carbon and nickel
to elements she will always seek to consume.

ORIGIN

What do you know of me?

The story remains the same
I traveled across land and sea
on the backs of infected rats
who carried infected fleas,
but my origin is much greater.

I am ancient, an existence long
since in place, far before you
read your books and looked
me up once, thinking you knew
facts from myths, from lies
but you know nothing.

Superstitious fools, refusing to even
look one another in the eyes lest
pestilence spread through aerial spirit
and what do the eyes of a sick man see
before he crosses over into darkness?

I cross boundaries,
continents will not contain me --
status, class, religion disappear
when I contaminate your present
obliterate your future
and consume society into dust.

In the end, sailors and monarchs
taste the same, and I will never
leave entirely, no vaccination
exists to empty my bacteria
forever from your world,
until then --

I sleep. I wait. I wonder...

What do the eyes of a sick man see
before he crosses over into darkness?

THE SIEGE OF CAFFA
(1346)

The use of disease as a weapon --
do not make the mistake of thinking
biological warfare
is only relevant in modern times.

When plague came for the Tartars,
claiming their bodies with swollen
armpits and groins, erupting orifices
with bile, blood, and phlegm,
devastating the army
with astonishing numbers of dead,
hope of overtaking Caffa vanished

but plans do not always need hope
sometimes all they need is vindictive
anger, a leader desperate enough
to command corpses be catapulted
across fortified walls, into the city's
heart, onto desperate citizens,
refuges, traitors and saints alike.

All victim to putrid stench of the dead,
all prey to infectious plague
sprouting from cadavers, visible sickness
even more deadly in its invisible
spread of bacteria from the hurl
of contagious bodies into Caffa.

When the army leaves, sick but maybe
also satisfied at having quenched
the hubris of their enemies, horror
beyond sight of crows feasting,
beyond stench of corpses rotting,
spreads through the city, through homes

21

and bodies -- others will blame rats,
Messina's ships, fleas, but what of war,
what of the wealthy lining their pockets
through risk and inevitable transmission
of a disease they do not yet have a name for,

what of dead bodies stacked like mountains
who the citizens must touch to be rid of,
besieged in battle and biological attack,
what of the many ships leaving Crimea,
taking over a year to even reach Europe,
bringing vectors of shore rats along
with all those merchants and soldiers?

The use of disease as a weapon --
perhaps only anecdotal in the end,
perhaps a horrifying account
that helped spread the plague only
in minor doses, but perhaps not.

Do not make the mistake of thinking
history will never repeat itself,
no matter how horrifying,
no matter the amount of dead,
and no matter the lies we tell ourselves.

Second Pandemic

Close the pubs, burn the mutts
cull the cats, ignore the rats

Wholesale massacre of the wrong
animals, no claws and fangs left
to eat the vermin who carry the fleas
all that's left is invitation to disease

Now plague spreads faster, dire
conditions brew dismal deaths
look there, beneath the old birch tree
new stack of bodies before I count to three

They blame miasma, blame the air
rancid bowels of earth beyond compare

Subtle, venomous, arising between feces
and all the waste you breed, sewer streets,
rotten meat, no escape even for the elite

Doom or omen, what sin have we brought
to our doors, what pestilence swam across
infected oceans to exterminate our shores,
and what must we do with all these bodies?

When Dorothy dies, we dig her grave,
share a drink and play a song, hum lullabies
for the dead, our communal lips cursed
only defeat and shared sickness dispersed,

but we didn't know, we didn't know
the way bacteria spread, the God-fearing
dread our only penance to be worthy, treat
neighbors better, stay away from acts of vanity
no bathing, no gambling, no drink, no vice

Close the pubs, burn the mutts
cull the cats, ignore the rats

Clean up the streets, but who is left?
The very breakdown of society reflected
in the misery of all locked inside
no sisters left for me to confide
that I saw the blacksmith kill a man
that I saw the priest wrap his hands
around our cousin's fair throat

The watchman will not let us out
my bribes all go unheard,
each night he burns brimstone
and amber, as if smoking out
infection will keep him atoned

There is no safety, no mercy left
no animals in the streets, only
awful screaming invades my ears
and bloody, hacking coughs on repeat

Close the pubs, burn the mutts
cull the cats, ignore the rats,
but what must we do with all these bodies?

DEATH SHIPS

In cold October twelve ships sail
churning through the deep Black Sea,
they do not arrive with broken masts
as they begin to dock in Sicily,

nor with blood dripping from the bow
or any other signs of disease,
but within the ships, sailors are dead
and those still alive find no mercy.

Upon inspection, Sicilian authorities uncover
corpses stacked in storage; sailors plead
for death as dark cysts ooze blood and pus,
too late for containment, the powers concede.

They send the death ships on their way,
chant prayers of their own to protect Messina
but it is too late, pestilence has arrived
and spreads with hunger like an infectious hyena.

Bodies continue to move from house to house
and business carries on within the city,
but bacteria feasts on innocent cells
as Black Death makes its mark on Sicily.

BREWED CONDITIONS

Hush falls over the port city,
gentle as lulling rain
before horrendous storm
takes over, drowning all
beneath hurricane rage

Summer of 1348, hope
disappears quick as striking
lightning against a tall tree,
splintering and burning
beneath a fiery reign

Filth flows in open ditches
as fish stink up the town
contaminated ale spilled
as trading meats turn brown

Well water grows polluted
sanitation but now a dream,
nothing left to find here
but wildfire disease

Thousands of souls crying
for help as their bodies swell
the grass outside grows taller
embracing the town in hell

Alone, the living cannot
bury the dead, and alone
they perish, too -- ruins
and remnants all that remain
beneath the plague's brew

Ruinous Halcyon

The world grows quiet
as pestilence arrives
even the wars have stopped --
is this what it takes,
indescribable deaths,
for peace to appear
amid a world
constantly rejecting
offers of harmony?

Rattus rattus

Little pest, scrambling
through the dark, black
coat blending into night,
nocturnal creature
and all his mates, hiding
aboard trader ships
within straw beds
beneath the pillows
of sailors' heads

R. rattus, squeaking
when threatened
when the men try
to chase it away
from their food,
already contaminated
too late, the vermin runs
leaves smears of oil
along moldy walls,
territorial marks

Rattus rattus, blamed
but only a small part
of a larger equation
in a time where human
lice and fleas
dance between bodies,
strands of hair,
each touch a quick
exchange of grim omens
to follow, of nights
much darker
than the rat's black coat.

CRIMSON MERCY

I paint red marks on her door -- a cross,
tall and long, a mockery of something holy
floating above the crooked words:
"Lord, have mercy on us"

As if the phrase could bring comfort
to sickly souls struggling for one more breath

Paint drips from the lettering, dark
droplets resemble blood clots
raining down until the blacksmith arrives
to lock her up, my intended bride, my bright star

She must reside within for now, for days,
if she can survive that long -- her family
waits with staggered coughs and swollen
boils, her brother dying and her parents
as pale as maggots wriggling across
rotting faces in burial pits where fires
have not yet been lit for the evening

Those locked inside houses are nothing
but servants of sickness who never stood
a chance to overcome such darkness
inside where no one will help her
because when fake comfort drips crimson
you cannot mistake it for rosy delusions
named hope, named religion, named anything
other than the pariah of life pestilence is

From parish to parish, the sickness came
took our people as most of the clergy left,
yet they insist we pay the church, beg for mercy --
clemency is a lie, drowning beneath sticky paint

I scoff at the idea of mercy as my lover screams,
as I receive a small glimpse of her withered body,
as the gravedigger comes at night to collect
her brother, her father, her mother, and then her,
all her color and life destroyed beneath stinking illness

A red cross on your door is not a sign of hope,
the words scribbled at the command of godly men
perpetuate lies, a condemnation for all within to die,
yet they do not think I understand the way death
lingers between the ruins of infectious households

I understand, and I have lost all hope, all love
so I paint red crosses on welded doors
knowing containment is a myth even as I dream
of real compassion at night, until the dawn breaks,

and it is time I paint my own red cross
before the blacksmith comes, but I will let him
lock me in -- I sit quietly when the reaper knocks,
when we stare at one another until the suffering
inside me consumes all gasping breaths of air

With a scythe at his side, he reaches for me,
black gloves stained in crimson mercy,
a ghoul who brings comfort, who brings death
at last, the only sanctuary to truly take us away
from the blasphemy and pain of this ailing earth

Moral Decay

Outside your door, dig a pole
into the ground, hang a bale of straw
when infection invites itself
inside your home; wait forty days

If you must leave, carry a white stick
notify others to stay away, death
follows -- you are a beacon, a warning

Do not give into moral meltdown
keep away from drink and bestial
appetites, do not allow evil's breath
to blow great sin across your soul

Decay of virtues summons pestilence
irrevocable wickedness found
within every satisfied human craving

Hang a bale of straw outside your door
do not come out, do not allow anyone in,
no matter how loud their knocking,
no matter how loud their screaming,
do not let anyone inside

Village Gravediggers

Father forgive me,
I burned mother's body
late last night
when the whole town slept,

except for us, we chosen few
who knock on your doors
who clean up your dead,
and father forgive me
I will have to burn you, too.

The poor remain,
and a few clergymen
a house full of children,
coughing, tightly locked in,
and if they try to run,

we must all chase them down.

Three weeks go by,
all my little brothers die,
will you weep for them, father,
when I light their grave flames?

When father finds the first bubo
swelling black on his thigh,
he prays to a god long since gone
and tries his best to escape, to run.

We all must chase him down.

I paint the doors, I dig the graves,
the blacksmith locks another family in.
Father, don't weep, don't breathe on me
save your energy for the reaper's judgment.

I'm too hungry to cry, too poor to eat
as I morph the last of my kin to ash.
Dig another bone pit, sing gospel songs
as another runner hits the ground,
bound away from locks no match for fear,

and we all must chase him down.

The Corpses Burn

Poison inside me, and I must scratch it out
I dig and dig through flesh, ripping
skin apart until wet strips hang from
my bones like I am a drying rack
for my own meat, but still the poison
stings, still the disease sharpens pain
through every muscle, fiber, and atom

I excavate nerves and organs until my heart
reveals itself behind the jailed protection
of a rib cage -- in there I will find the toxins,
in there each beat sends a command
to my brain, allowing this fever, this darkness
permeation through my aching existence

Baptized in each metallic drop of blood
I pray to nothing when my body collapses,
when at last freedom takes me away from
venomous husks I must call home, and each
inhale breathes in scorched human meat
burning through burial pits where even in hell,
there is not enough room for all our dead bodies

Divine Punishment

I am not forgiven,
but still I pray.

Dear God, my family
has not been spared
two children dead,
one sick with boils
with blackened fingers
and toes like soot,

my wife taken
by the village gravedigger
to be burned in a pit
like all the others.

When her debris ascends,
I pray you forgive her
and deliver her to our children
who must surely be safe
beneath your bright light.

I am not forgiven,
but still I pray.

My life of greed
I repent it now,
my sin of adultery
I repent it now,

yet I wonder,
have all the townsfolk
sinned in your eyes,
has every dead child
not earned your love?

Why must we all end
alone with our terror?

I am not forgiven,
but still I pray.

FLAGELLANTS

Finely dressed men arrived at midday,
stood in the center of town with arms
held wide, as if to embrace our fear

They removed crinkled white shirts,
invited townspeople to understand
God's wish for penance, for punishment

Leather straps in hand, knotted in the middle
with sharp needles or metal within; the men
grin and pray, make sure we watch closely

The ritual repeats three times a day
as they scar their own bodies, invite us
closer to watch, to join, to beg forgiveness

For thirty-three days, they bleed,
backs and chests morph into shredded
skin ribbons, then they move onward

The next town is greeted the same way,
those of us left behind succumb to illness
wondering if the flagellants brought plague

along with forced atonement; these fanatics
continue in the face of papal resistance,
the church will not allow this to continue

Bleed, scream, pray, punish -- repeat,
death listens, but does not care
just as God listens, but does not care.

Princess Joan

Gown of red velvet
royally wrapped around
her body, diamonds
glittering as the procession
takes her onward, toward
marriage, toward union
between England and Castile

Dear Princess, jewels
will not save you
from infection,
nor can one hundred bowmen
offer true protection

Daughter of Edward III,
no stranger to the ruthlessness
charisma can hide, but she
holds her head high, fears
nothing on this day despite
warnings from the townsfolk
of disease drawing nearer

Dear Princess, an entire
ship needed for your dowry
will not keep you from disease,
in this matter more than deadly
stay home, we beg you, please

Too late, your lethal timing
cannot be stopped by fine
enamel buttons, by patterns
of shining stars in corsets, nor by
embroidered roses or gold combs
no matter how beautiful you look,
death still comes, dear Joan

The lion of your monarchy roars
one last time before sickness finds
you, strikes the leader of your entourage
dead, sniffs you out like vermin
seeking scraps because all is not well
in Bordeaux, and the Black Death
spares no mercy for royalty

Dear Princess, we begged you so
but you have come to die with us,
rest by the corpses piled on the dock
and in good faith you trust,
but your body will not be shipped back
in time to your broken father

You will burn with the villagers
fine wedding gown forgotten
for all skeletons look the same
when remains become rotten

ᗪANSE ᗰACABRE

"What you are, we were; what we are, you shall be."

The mirror phrase, yes come tell me,
do you know it? Have you heard it?

Death will level you, king or servant.

Hide in darkness, dance in light
close your eyes or keep them wide
death comes silent, an unannounced plight

children hold hands with butchers
popes bow to laborers
blacksmiths smile at lords,
and queens embrace the farmers.

All will glide together
between fruitless trees, where the dead and living
come to speak alternately --

look upon us, we skeletons in glassy lake reflections,
search between beauty and terror and bones
to find your own skin shimmering back with
infections.

Danse unites us all, through plague, famine, and war
twirl and sweat until escape taunts you,
just beyond the crimson sand of hell's shore

Do you know it? Have you heard it?

Death will level you, king or servant.

BLOODLETTING

Crude methods for poisonous disease,
bloodletting and boil-lancing
unsanitary danger covered up
like illusion by aromatic herbs
burning, sending smoke to a heaven
long since abandoned by broken
people; come bathe in rosewater,
in vinegar, pretend the practice
of bleeding a vein's hot blood
will save you from plague-ravaged
hell, will save you from anything
other than the truth of your dying.

The King's Ulcer

His calves were once the finest, dear Henry VIII,
strong, powerful muscle displayed by a garter
fastened above the knee, a young man intent
on ruling with the same greatness shown
throughout his sportsman adventures—
tennis and jousting, never a worry about the slight
swelling, the *throb-throb-throb* of something beating
itself into life beneath the flesh of his thigh.

The prowess of jousting will come with a cost,
severe injuries growing worse as he confesses
the ulcer and its *throb-throb-throb* blistering
beneath his leg; how to heal this king who will not
listen to the doctors, who will not give up hordes
of wine and meat, deterioration is inevitable,
and dear Henry VIII, the stench of putrid rot
travels through the rooms now, announcing his
arrival before they even see his morbid body
waltzing through golden doors on restless legs,

bandaged tight to keep the pus inside, but everyone
knows what the *throb-throb-throb* echoing throughout
the castle means that dear Katharine, the last wife,
will become his nurse, will watch and assist
doctors as they lance ulcers with pokers burned
hot from hellfire to sizzle against infection,
still it will never be enough to save the king.

Even when they carry him around his palace,
hoisting the mass of him above their heads, not blinking
as bouts of fever sweat down his head and drip,
but they will hear the screams later as leg ulcers
are cauterized, as discharge and blood ooze out
together in blackened swirls, charred like hot tar

and the *throb-throb-throb* of what beat beneath
the king's ulcer will beat no more.

Scapegoat

How far will people in power go?
There are no limits, no boundaries
when fear and hate mingle,
when forced confessions
leave souls stained in scarlet drowning

Propaganda propels anger
toward persecution, toward raging
flames consuming innocent hearts
still alive when the fires are set,
and Strasbourg will not forget
such pain, the bodies floating
in wine casks down the river Rhine
will not forget undeserved torment
at the hands of Christian loathing

The aftermath of plague will not
excuse you, and your God will not
excuse you from crimson stains
spotted beneath fingernails, from the
soul still drowning in all that blood

Memento Mori

Remember that you will die,
don your darkest clothes
or your brightest
whatever brings you peace
as we practice the art of mourning

Seek salvation for your soul
reflect upon your goodness,
your sins, see here the way
art changed after
Great Pestilence,
how paintings depict
villagers staring death
straight in the face,
how they pull their sleeves
away from the grip of demons

To live and die well
you may show your face
to the world, a statue
on one side reflecting wealth
in smiles and fine clothes,
but on the back, *finis*, the end
reflecting only skeletal grins,
a corpse drowning in frogs,
worms, slithering salamanders
seeking nutrients from your
body, your mortality

Remember that you will die,
so that you do not forget to live.

LAMENTATION

My beloved friends, all gone
their sweet faces I see no more,
what lightning has struck
and burnt their joys to ashen gore?

It is no storm that has drowned them
nor an abyss to swallow bodies whole,
but this great pestilence of sorrow
that has reaped a most deadly toll.

Such pain, merely the beginning
of sorrow and prolonged mourning,
I wonder if I lament in vain
as plague takes souls without warning

I write to my brother,
who proves to be alive
the rest of his monastery dead,
only he and his dog survive

I fear the entire world aches
from this evil's sweeping pain,
what good, what truth will arise
from this, as we all lament in vain?

ABSOLVED

Forgive me, love
I cannot resist
crawling toward
your body, even
in death I must
have your skin
touching my skin,

your lips caressing
my lips, even your
abscesses spilling
discharge and foul blood
into my own punctured
pustules leaking down
my naked body

Forgive me, love
with my arms
wrapped around you,
the boils on my thighs
grating against open
sores aflame on your
groin before sickness
takes me into the dark,
let me have you,
one last time, let me
taste your plague

IN THE BUTCHERED AFTERMATH

Cruelness is nothing new, the women know --
the Great Pestilence brought great death,
babies are sparse, and laborers too

To sustain a butchered population, the women
must produce, must fulfill both roles
of babymaker and worker
of productive and docile,
yet nothing seems to be good enough

They hear tales of royal women, fierce creatures
expected to produce heirs, but who also match
their rivals, lord and rule over the men,
ladies capable of commanding armies
while they hold a baby in their arms

But the women know history will not be kind
to their sisters, will be written by jealous cowards
who twist strength into hysteria
who paint pictures of greed while blood stains
their own hands from past wars and slaughter

Cruelness is nothing new, the women know.

"And now was acknowledged the presence of the Red Death. He had come like a thief in the night. And one by one dropped the revellers in the blood-bedewed halls of their revel, and died each in the despairing posture of his fall. And the life of the ebony clock went out with that of the last of the gay. And the flames of the tripods expired. And Darkness and Decay and the Red Death held illimitable dominion over all."

- Edgar Allan Poe, *The Masque of the Red Death*

Seven Rooms

Patterns from stained glass wander across stone floors
designs stretch like a phantasmagoric yawn, never static
within the prince's castle as the revelers dance,
and though the glass is strong, it will not keep me out.

Royalty celebrates life, believing they are safe,
far away from the dark death which ravages alleyways
and poverty-stricken hearts below his majesty's hill,
but the "white radiance of eternity" as Shelley once wrote,
is not found here -- colored glass forms not a dome, but a cage.

Seven rooms of different colors intent to strike confusion,
such walls may blind me in blue, purple, green madness,
may deceive me in orange, white, violet embraces,
but you will always end up in a black room with scarlet panes
and though the glass is strong, it will not keep me out.

Plead for salvation as the ebony clock tolls on,
as midnight fast approaches wrought upon your fear
flames expire and party guests collapse, each citizen
of the prince's court, and the prince himself, fall victim.

All these hideous and fatal moments, run if you like,
find each room jeweled in dewdrops of blood,
pray for colorful patterns to hide you within deception
and though the glass is strong, it will not keep me out.

CRADLELAND OF PARASITES

You will walk in blood after the birth
and the very violence of such a thing,
how an origin shreds through membrane
how copper stains your lips and tongue,
will terrorize each atom in your body.

Sickness has always been here,
waiting in light and dark, hovering
in your air, and swimming through
each breath and drop of water,

did you ever think something as microscopic
as a germ could hurt this much?

You will take my hand when the air aches
when clouds have only acid lakes to absorb,
before your organs break down into dust
before life exits your body in an angry burst,
shut your eyes, tell me what bacterium curses you.

In the cradleland of parasites, beginnings
are always brutal, the way plague rips
venomous disease from contagion's womb
spilling her gore across a vermillion wasteland,

does love still exist in this place where flesh
spills open and the maggots come to feast?

You will walk in blood after the birth,
taste spores sprouting through atmosphere,
remember the origin must always be violent
remember humankind will not survive this,
we will rebuild our cradleland from their bones.

51

1665

The Great Pestilence has risen again,
Spring brings no rosy blooms this year
just a reminder of plague and sin.

Hotter days attract more fevered deaths,
as streets littered in rubbish welcome
rats to come builds nests of warm sewage.

Between insufferable pain,
violent headaches, and bursting buboes
that stab torment through the skin,

there are those who walk on --
silently infectious as contagious ghosts
spreading their haunted air onward.

The townspeople will hope, pray, bleed
out into the arms of masked doctors
who faintly smell of wildflower herbs.

Bills of Mortality

Down the alley and across the yard,
the note is tacked for all to see
it costs only a penny to publish
all these bills of mortality

Some die from consumption
others from age or grief,
this week two died from colic
and one body was found on the street

Next week on Thursday morning,
when the bill is again revealed
a cause we have not seen in years
unleashes panic once concealed

The front page is a bleak reminder
of the death we are propelled near
skeletons dance around the edges,
ink flaking and smeared

Beneath causes of fever and fright,
above rupture, scurvy, and teeth
plague looms with growing numbers
set to increase by one thousand next week

King Charles has fled, along with the rich
as death flourishes with obscene cravings,
the poor and damned will try to leave
starving, wretched, and without savings

Certificates of health are denied
exodus morphs into condemned dread
by September hope is lost then burned
as the bill posts for the week: 7,000 dead

Down the alley and across the yard,
there is barely anyone alive to see
the note tacked against the wall
where plagues rewrites our history

Bubonic Litany

Almost tender at first,
freckle-sized spots
from me to you
little love bites
as fleas cascade
down like dying eyelashes

make a wish, darling.

They call me pandemic
and blame the heavens,
riot against clouds
accuse the very air hovering
around, but my miasma
digs deeper into the dirt
of filthy, human secrets.

I sing you a plaguing love song
as masked men arrive, a covenant
of fake doctors with ill intent,
stuffing aromatic rose petals, juniper,
lemon, mint, spices inside their beaks,
all hiding from my putrid breath
as their canes poke your boiling skin
saying, *let me in.*

I am bubonic on your tongue,
dance with me beneath melting, gray skies
as you swell up, apple-sized raindrops
bulge beneath your flesh,
longing to burst, ooze pus and blood,
contaminate those pecking beaks
before your flesh darkly rots, falls off,
and this is me trying to find a way inside you.

Fever and crimson vomit,
do you hear the rats, sweet little pathogens,
scurrying after you?
Harbor me in your lungs
(two to seven days, then you're mine)
every haggard breath is my affection
contaminating mortality,
are the boils on your groin
too much love?
Just trying to dig in deep
with parasitic hands and teeth,
let me in.

Each patch of purple skin
glimmers wetly on your body,
slick bruises from my grip
aching and clinging for you to just
let me in.

Come with me
before you are left behind,
discarded to deal with the fervor
of what I leave in my wake,
away from the religious fanatics
who will bloom dandelion-quick
and blame the living
for the dead,
cut and burn each other.

Let me love you,
carry you away in the embrace
of millions of others
because everyone is a leper in the end,
and the only plague vaccine
is to give in.

I am Black Death
and I'd say once again to let me in,

but here I am
beneath your heart's withered shadows,
within your marrow's rust
clutching your carcass
in pestilence's last embrace.

Brokers of the Dead

The streets wane into emptiness
silence weighs like a heavy curtain
smothering all those padlocked inside
homes of sickness and rot, of agony

Children watch their parents die
coughing blood onto ragged clothes
praying for rescue, for salvation
but all that answers are men in overcoats,
poking at dead bodies with wooden canes
examining the sick with beaked heads
cocked to the side while one pockets
coins found in a carcass's apron

When the plague doctor comes
crawl under the bed, take a breath
hold it in, don't breathe, don't move --
if they find you, you'll be locked
inside until you die, just like the others

When the plague doctor comes
you could open your veins, bleed
out your family, your own body
for the same results produced
by these menacing figures, oh
when the plague doctor comes
kill your mother, your sister,
yourself for the same outcomes

These brokers of the dead,
grave creatures who carry no cure
only mislabeled vials, useless
no matter how hard you pray,
the plague doctor comes
tips his leather hat to another

doctor in the street, breathes in
rose petals stuffed in his beak,
moves along as if nothing is wrong
because what else can he do for you?

PREVENTATIVE MEASURES

Dissolve opium in brandy,
wear protective amulets
beneath the armpit

Smoke tobacco,
eat lettuce

Provide alcohol and opium
brews even for the children

Drink fine wine,
pray to God

If feeling ill, take a chicken
pluck it clean, apply live
chicken to swollen nodes,
animal will absorb sickness;
repeat until chicken
or patient dies

Sit next to hot fire,
sweat out illness
disease will travel in air
to nearest sewage area

For swellings and boils
apply paste of gum resin
roots of white lilies
and dried excrement

You might also seek out
ground unicorn horn,
crushed emeralds --
do not substitute
with mercury or arsenic

Blackbirds, Black Death

Blackbirds outside my window
have you come to take me away?
My sister is dying, but together we waste
and count the days, the days, the days...

I'd rather follow you into the skies
away from choking black smoke,
away from dark soil where death blooms
on grotesque petals and charcoal stems
swell until blood drips down the stalks.

Bells sing distorted songs in the distance
chiming again for departed souls, striking
melodies against the harsh growl of thunder,
but sister still dies, crinkled like a lifeless spider
in my arms, for she is dead, and I am dead
in this place the blackbirds call home.

When blackbirds come to drain my blood,
their beaks stuffed with straw and juniper
I offer my eyes as penance for sin, to combat
God's severance, but we are despised,
left nothing but rot, and ruin, and rats.

When blackbirds come to take her away at last,
we decompose together, imprinted memories
stain childhood blankets, infection reeks
from frayed threads as doctors dressed in black
pretend they are birds, but it is too late,
and I no longer count the days, the days, the days...

We twine together and choke, smoldering embers
of our home reach across the floor
colored in our bloodletting, yet the smoke
smells like mint as the blackbirds retreat,

and we will never follow them into the skies.

Because when blackbirds come, they are but men
buttoned up in masks, coats, and presumptions
that they know better, they know a cure,
but they know nothing except death,
the scent of putrid bodies mixed with herbs,
the swelling of buboes before they burst.

Sister, we once planted imaginary gardens
for imaginary birds, but now blackbird men
have materialized from that secret place
and stand guard outside my window,
have they come to take me away?

Dear sister is dead, so together we waste
and count the days, the days, the days...

Yersinia pestis

A hunter went to skin his prize
opening up the carcass with care,
blood and meat drip down
scarlet rivulets seeking the breaks
in his flesh, small cuts and wounds
not quite healed, raw enough
for bacteria to slip inside
like bees into a hidden hive

He breathes in the odor of earthy
game meat, tasting copper promises
of stew and hearty meals to come,
fleas hop from dead fur to live skin
leaving bites only noticeable
with the slightest of itches

Infection carries in his lungs
when he goes to kiss his wife,
she brings the venison to the table
and together the family dines;
droplets hover in the air
when he holds his children tight
not knowing deadly infection
was also bidding them goodnight

48 SKELETONS

Last rites are not afforded here,
no way to lay the dead peacefully
no token of familial love, just bodies,
and the clothes they died in.

Mass burials become a sign
of a broken system, the community
cannot cope, families cannot wait
for a priest, for a gravedigger.

There is only the pit, where 48
bodies are arranged carefully
side by side in eternal slumber,
until nothing remains but bones,
and the clothes they died in.

ᏢEST ᏁOUSE

The first is hastily built, a wooden
shack resting at the town's edge,
an uninviting structure where wind
whistles through the gaps, cold tendrils
gripping the sick with frosty fingers,
feverish confusion tormenting unwell
minds just before death takes over.

Within, screams of pain echo throughout
corridors and bedchambers, the sharp odor
of human waste stings the air in wasp-like
viciousness -- a reminder of inescapable
humiliation as victims are too weak to move,
too tired to do anything but sweat into sheets
and beg for something akin to relief, but
such a wish will only arrive with death's howl.

Within, the women take on dangerous work,
fiercely lancing buboes only to be blamed
for the disease's spread as if their own
hands created its noxious poisons;
the nurses will be called wicked by others
who do not yet have the science to understand,
who not yet have the compassion to listen.

Behind the house, families burn,
all who die from infection disposed
quickly in rapid fire, thick smoke
the choking odor of scorched,
melting flesh tainting the air
as skin crisps and fat liquifies,
as hair blackens and bones remain
sturdy in the earth, charred evidence
quietly telling the story of plague.

Necrosis

Septicemic plague
one of three,
but this is the one
where your fingers darken
where your nose turns rotten

Purpuric lesions
arrive after the fever
as if summoning sin
to rise with flesh, be present
beneath the surface

Recurrent nightmare
spreading demise through
body horror like no other,
you are betrayed
and I am betrayed
by this thing we cannot name

Later they will discover
bacteria and corpses,
relics like ancient breadcrumbs
leading them to name
our suffering like a song,
Black Death, little Black Death --
the melody that killed us all.

MECCA OF INFECTION

Into the poison land I journey
cloak wrapped tight, leather mask
binding my face, fusing lips together
ragged paper and quill in hand
stories staring up at me from haunted
faces locked in houses, from mountains
of bodies amassed by the docks

No deliverance in the mecca of infection,
no person willing to come forth and tell
their story less they bring plague back
to families sheltered away inside, but
still I write of skies so gray, of rivers
stagnant in filth and grime, no birds
sing except the carrion eaters, no bells
toll except the ones at dusk, warning
of death and burials during starless night

With careful distance and measured steps,
I follow the strange doctors into homes
where townspeople writhe, blood droplets
form at the corners of mouths, pierced boils
trickle down sweat-covered arms, I watch,
I write, and they die -- repeat, repeat, repeat

It never ends, never stops in the mecca,
only death thrives, summoning phantoms
constantly to cross over the souls of damned
persons, and no matter how fast I scribble,
I cannot depict the grim horror, the shattering
screams of agony, the wretched sight of life
leaving a mother's face, a son's body --
liberation from this curse becomes nothing more
than a hopeful dream I pen in my journals

MEDICO DELLA PESTE

This will pass as medicine, for now
morbid work must always exist,
but how much death will God allow?

We haunt the streets, blackbirds on the prowl,
seeking out hacking coughs, lumps, and cysts;
this will pass as medicine, for now.

Overcoat soaked in suet, a belief to somehow
repel plague's lure, its miasma in the air like mist,
but how much death will God allow?

Wooden cane in hand, we walk and they howl
patients broken by hellish agony plague enlists;
this will pass as medicine, for now.

Bound to remedy and coin, we must disavow
conspiracies set forth by the traitors in our midst
but how much death will God allow?

Between bloodied beaks, we turn and bow
complimenting each doctor the infection missed;
this will pass as medicine, for now,
but how much death will God allow?

Scorched

From the outskirts of my city's heart,
I stand and watch the cathedral burn
firestorm ravages humanity, merciless
with cruel flames gutting thousands
of houses, driving out fractions from
our already dwindling population

Humans and fleas and rats alike
flee the fanning blaze as it spreads
from the bakery and across London,
perhaps taking the last of great death
away on their vermin-tainted breath

From the outskirts of my city's heart,
I stand and wonder why -- why God
punishes with disease and inferno;
the plague was on the decline, at last,
but now we burn, unforgiven in hellfire

ᴅEATH ᴋNELL

We only bury the dead at night,
but even darkness cannot cover
such horrific mutilation found
upon the deceased's epidermis

Listen for the bells, sweet ringing
telling the story of unimagined dread,
gravediggers howl as they bury
family members, painful yowling
between the clanging of the bells,
the resounding warning of the bells
for surely this is hell plagued upon us

You must stay away from the bells
the feared screaming of the bells
or surely this hell will take you

Each burial grows longer, more time
needed to cover broken bodies
beneath cold earth's final resting tomb,
and all this time they do not stop
their clamor, each monotone ring
striking fright within melancholy melody

You must stay away from the bells
the despair twanging from the bells
and each death knell a never-ending
reminder of nightmares ringing true

We only bury the dead at night,
but it's just a matter of time
before your own bells ring, before
your own knell sings, and hell
takes you to the grave to pay your due

Shrouded Dreams

Dear mind, I beg of you
keep them away from my dreams
tonight I will take anything
no matter how grim or obscene,

terrorize me with poverty
or visions of executions so grim,
but brain I plead to your mercy
do not make me dream of them

those great skeletons veiled in white
they terrorize my soul,
when they dance around my grave
in dreams, I no longer have control

my heart beats into erratic fear
commanding my breath to stop,
for surely the end grows near
and I hear the blisters on my skin pop

the skeletons they come for me
weighty bones piercing into sores,
they climb out of misted dream clouds
rattling toward me on all fours

fearsome terrors yet I beg you still
dear mind please take them away,
give me doctors with black masks
or poison disguised in flasks,
but of skeletons veiled in white, oh dreams
you send me to the grave to decay

With Pestilence on Your Breath

I bury my family
within muddy tombs,
watch you do the same
from across the graveyard
choked with corpses
nothing but bones
and dying grass blades
separating our burials

walk to me
through fog,
pestilence on your breath,
in your blood,
crunch skulls beneath
your heavy steps
weighted down by agony
only I understand

because there is no cure
no veil of religion
that will shield
our bodies from disease

walk to me
bring your coughs,
your fever, kiss me
with polluted lips
before we join our kin
in the dirt ocean of death

After Angels Walk Through Blood

Silence suffocates
as I tread through the village,
ruin and devastation --
the only music that's survived,
disintegration of sound, of laughter

What do I compose after this,
what ballad or sonata will ever
compete with mud-thick
strangulation of emptiness
found in every home I glance in?

This void, this quiet
only after angels walk
through blood could there be
silence as profoundly choking
as the acidic one boiling within
my stomach lining,
every decaying corpse I meet
pointing a skeletal finger at me,
questioning how did *you*
survive, you man of music,
you wasteful thief of breath?

The bakers are dead, the farmers
and clergy, the women are gone,
children burned in the burial pit,
but I the composer carry on
stepping through cloying air
searching for life, for a melody,
for instruments to heal my heart,

but what do I compose after this,

what hymn will blood-soaked angels
hum along to as they hold wraithlike
bodies of villagers in their arms?

Island of Ghosts

Into the Venetian lagoon, we sail
where a small landmass welcomes
us to hell; every trodden ashen step
betrays the secrets madmen kept

Barges hauled the dead and exiled,
anyone displaying symptoms
no matter how mild -- welcomed to
the haunted isle where fire rages

Workers piled the dead in mass graves,
those too sick to move met similar fates
buried alive, burned while groaning
cremated to gray dust, to the very soil
billowing up beneath our footprints

Nowhere to run, victims could only swim
or wait to die within fiery embraces,
no escape except into the grave, for days
and days the bodies came, even washed up
along the coast, where plague victims
appeared as ghosts, dressed in singed clothes,
welcoming all to their festering island

REPERCUSSIONS OF RUIN

What comes after all of this,
in the quiet of the night when stars
shine again, sparkling in the sky
constant reminders of life's gifts,
what comes after all of this?

Beyond death's strongest waves,
small rays of light appear, flickering
throughout decimated villages
where people must rebuild, relearn
how to live in the repercussions of ruin

Such people grow stronger, live longer
than so many others before, enjoy years
their body never imagined experiencing,
create art and music and fashion
that never would have reached cultural
periods of rebirth if such tragedy
never staked its claim first in their lineage

Transition brings difficulties, smothers
flames into darkness, but when people
reignite warmth and light, when they
remember possibility for something new
and great to take the place of slaughtered
opportunities, then what comes after
all of this, can bring insurmountable beauty

An Advanced Society

Come with me now
away from feudal times
into the twenty-first century
where surely we are advanced,
where surely infectious disease
can be dealt with properly

Or maybe the danger still exists,
a public health challenge
prevailing past capabilities
of arrogant people who ignore
the severity and variety
transmitting from the world
as viruses jump to humans

I can only invite you to look,
observe a changing world
from your own perspective
but the rest, is it up to you,
or to people in power
who would sooner return us all
to medieval corruptions?

Caution: Germ Laboratory

Down into Plum Gut Harbor
the mostly empty boat sails,
thick fog obscures vision
as the ferry horn sounds

We invite you temporarily
to observe what happens here,
sign the affidavit, please,
and no photographs allowed

No contact with the livestock,
cattle, swine, deer, and goats
and please keep in mind
this is necessary, if you happen
across any slit throats

Remember we're doing good
here, studying virus and vaccine,
remember we are needed
no matter what you may see

Restricted Area

I went searching for the world's edge
and found an island, eight hundred acres
untamed, uncared for -- a sign reads
Restricted: Dangerous Animal Diseases

Wild thorns, hungry for new skin to rake
needled edges across, greet the traveler
who finds this mystery; hungrier still
are legions of ticks eager to feast
on any flesh that dares walk through
jungles of bursting green foliage

This spit of land, what stories and secrets
remain buried beneath tainted soil, within
polluted air from burning bodies stoking
black clouds to plume into air, visible
nightmares coalescing with blue sky

Yet I cannot run because poison ivy
snares my ankles as if to say, *I warned you*
knowing the rash will be the least
of my worries if I dare continue, if I push
onward to answer the venomous riddles
Plum Island has invited me to solve

OUTBREAK

Biosafety level three,
does that make you feel
comfortable when you leave
at night? The stench of dead
cattle fresh in your nostrils,
tortured meat having found
its way into your brain despite
all that protective wear

Viruses have escaped
from at least one lab,
what other germs seeped
through the air, and where
have they all gone?

In Building 62, madness
seizes the steers, mouths
foaming and healthy cells
liquefying -- pus accepts
incitements to swell inside
blisters, painful ulcers
accelerate into the mouth,
leaving nothing but bursting
agony as the animals ail,
waste away into corpses

Will we call this the greater
good, a necessary study of
slaughter, a means to an end
rooted in mass disposal?

Kill Day comes quickly now,
more frequently, infected bodies
dead or barely alive hauled in
by the cartload -- and you can dare

breathe air in after incinerators
stop burning, but the great rot
cemented in your mind will
follow you home, always,
until the next disease,
until the next outbreak,
but your hands will always be
stained in scarlet remembrance

ʟAB 257

What happens in the after,
when the place is shut down
when no scientists or vets
are left to deal with bacteria
hovering in the air, with
decaying animal remnants?

The gulls might still come,
hunting for shelter as storms
approach, finding only disease
just as gray harbor seals
might still come, foraging
for food amidst untouched nature
only to ingest kernels of contagion

Consequences are brushed off,
matters for others to deal with
for Mother Earth to fight against
as if she wouldn't learn to adapt,
to send her living kingdoms forth
drinking up evolution from blighted
islands and ocean and atmosphere

but maybe this time, humans are left
behind, maybe this time she will
understand the warfare brewing
within greedy minds, and leave them
with the same lungs -- breathing in
all that they infected and wrecked,
absorbing what happens in the after
as their marrow rots into the same ashy
soil where all their test subjects burned

Spillover

Humanity -- our dense forest
of bodies, bone-tinder dry
ready for kindling flame
to take hold, spread sick fires
throughout our population
ashen tongues misspeak,
attempt to blow out pathogens
jumping from animal species
into human blood, outbreak
becomes a household term
as we all breathe in charred
scents of burning leaves

pretend acrid, rich odor
smells normal, but normality
reflects only in the natural world
masquerading as a reservoir
for human disease; we pretend
landfills and deforestation, habitat
destruction and toxic waste dumping
keeps us profitable, are necessary,
but false notions create false securities
until spillovers break through barriers
burrow inside and name you host
burning your kindling body to dust

RABID

Bullet-shaped, as if its lethality
has never been any secret
crawling centimeter by centimeter
toward the brain, warping
the mind into fatally crushing
rationale as it spurs aggression
into overdrive, the great heat
unspooling thoughts, sticky
salivation slobbering foam
from pursed lips and sharp teeth;
demonic in nature, this virus
of the nervous system -- possession
may form in the wild or the domestic,
turning once loved companions
into deadly, infectious strangers

Love in the Time of Sickness

Love in the time of sickness,
how do we feed our needs?
With dishes full of white maggots,
or simply surrendering to disease?

Purity-seekers will call it holy,
these angel-colored servings
where the devil dwells beneath
putrid food, sending parasites
through bowls and into bowels.

We transmute love into death,
asking the air to donate life
or sustenance, but all we can do
is suck bacteria between our lips,
swallow each hazardous breath
down into intestines where maggots
named after love will forever haunt
diseased bodies, these blessed specters
squirming between marrow until
our dying day skulks into our skulls.

Love in the time of sickness,
nothing but a fevered dream --
there are no needs to fulfill
when all we loved is buried
beneath our crawling knees,
desperately digging down,
down, down into dirt for bodies,
for maggots, for one last good meal
until the gravediggers arrive.

Between Lifeforms

The tale as old as time
is not one of romance,
but one of the balance
between lifeforms --

how alteration of environments
is as ancient as all preceding
lifeforms, present and extinct.

The delicate, yet powerful
balance, the reliance
on an ecosystem
that would thrive better,
that will thrive better
when humanity ceases
its polluted footprint

when the web of life
sticks to slick skin
casts flesh into parasitic fields,
where insects and vultures
join passively to feed
to restore delicate
blades of grass to natural beauty,

and to commit all herbivores
into meat-eaters just long enough
to rid the planet of its human disease.

GENOME

I have asked the bacteria inside me
for a name, for a lineage
it does not answer, instead shows
blurred curves as if defining
something so ancient could
only result in clouded answers

I shred through my genome
searching for a complete set
of sequences to recode DNA
without bacteria and virus,
to eliminate protein gained
during birth from my mother's
bloodstream; I demand to start
over, to swallow mitochondria
into a yawning black maw of abyss
and restructure my body
like Frankenstein's monster

I am my own necromancer --
erasing all I have accumulated
bringing a body back as blank,
perfect nothingness waiting
on evolution, waiting on your
destruction and resurrection,
blending our genetic structures
together because there is no
us versus them, there is only
mixing and morphing, DNA
shifting within all that we are

When My Lover Gives Birth to Plague

When my lover gives birth to plague
her twisted spine warps further, sending
seizures to coil around her bones,
perverse contractions as boils burst
allowing pus to seep down sallow skin
where diseased fleas bathe in her sickness

When my lover gives birth to plague
black rats swim from her broken water,
travel down a blood canal after gnawing
through her raw uterus, tasting the cervix
as a cherry treat for their months spent
engorged inside her pustule-covered belly

When my lover gives birth to plague
infestation spreads with mucus-covered mayhem
seeking out every crevice of flesh to wedge
dark globs of gangrene horror beneath,
to morph skin into rotting froths, fizzing off
skeletons who once had names, homes, lives…

but when my lover gives birth to plague
there is no escape, no hiding one's self
from omnipotent pathogens come to collect
what is promised; all the ruin and devastation,
all the science and medicine in the world won't
protect you when pestilence breaks free of its womb

Life Forms

I am destruction in your lungs,
invader of cells, assembling
genetic mutations to command
collapse of your willing body

I am creation, viral evolution
ancient and complex, storing
information for every virulent
level of transmission

Find water, and you'll find me
in an oozing handful of mud
cascading from roaring waterfalls
buried beneath arctic ice, forever
intertwined with life and death

Schistosomiasis

Neglected tropical disease
but I neglect nothing
when it comes
down, down, down
to inviting your body
out for parasitic dates
where the afterglow revolves
around wriggling such filth
deep into desecrated ground

Second only to malaria
in terms of my devastation
come here and wriggle
down, down, down
where cercariae bloom
from freshwater snails
and dance along the current
searching for contact, for skin
for how sweet your flesh tastes

How does the water stay fresh
after contamination spreads,
after disease falls
down, down, down
and mere days later I develop
beneath rash and itch,
within fever and muscle aches
waiting as my eggs travel
through your liver and bladder

Your body reacts, begs
for your nails to ply open
stomach walls and reach
down, down, down
into my dark cavern,

scoop out parasitic worms
latched onto your juicy insides,
but I neglect nothing
and leave you in hollow lambency

A Universal Constant

Everywhere, and in all things
unavoidable, inescapable
beyond the circle of communal
experiences, shared sickness,
there will always be new germs,
unfound bacteria, inner parasites
who do not yet have names
changing strains and mutating,
evolving to the world we created,
an eternal present and future
everywhere, and in all things.

HERD IMMUNITY

What good am I
when vaccinations stop,
when the public no longer believes
in the possibility of something bubonic,
something riddled with death
that extends like connective lightning
from body to body to body.

What good am I
when the planet burns,
when ancient contagions are released
into a searing atmosphere intent
on destroying greedy humans
who refuse to understand
how I will spread and spread and spread.

What good is safety in numbers
when the numbers decline,
when I can no longer protect you
because you don't believe in me
even though infection reveals mutated
remnants of broken worlds,
showing you its forgotten bodies.

What good am I
when the question no longer
revolves around me, but switches
truths to ask what good are you?

How will you ever protect anyone
from infectious hunger like this,
when you never bothered to shield
the sick and compromised immune systems
around you for the sake of misinformation?

What good are you
when the last body falls,
when tiny lungs of children breathe no more;
even I will not outlast the final virus,
together in death's contagious arms
we weep and weep and weep.

INHABITED

The human body
never alone, colonized
since birth by bacteria

one thousand times
smaller than a pencil tip
adapting with our growth

learning our unique cells
like a language only
microbiota can speak

semantics of protection
or great destruction
offer the same promise

the human body
never alone, colonized
daily by bacteria

WITH THE WORM IN HER HEAD

She loses syllables at first,
as if her lips refused to form
a's and oh's, later in the day
whole words disappear.

At first, it's a tumor
glowering back at her
from the films of CT scans,
an accusing lesion
in the left frontal area.

She slides into the MRI scanner
like a stiff body into the morgue,
claustrophobic terror weighing
her down, or maybe it's embalming fluid
either way the nightmare remains.

Many doctors and consultations later
one introduces her to a new word,
cysticercosis --

inside her brain, the worm did whisper
from where it has lived for nearly six years,
from where it has tried to produce its own eggs,
a hermaphrodite fertilizing life, cementing spawn
to flow down the blood river inside her body.

She takes her medicine to kill the tapeworm,
to end its campaign of potential eggs
living on within her body,
to stop the continuations of whispers
in her brain, to take back the words
she desperately needs to live her life,
to speak her mind.

So many of us host parasites unknowingly,
hoping they live as communal feeders
dining at the table of our organs
without inflicting infection or harm,
but sometimes they start to whisper
and travel beneath our skin,
sometimes they steal our syllables, at first,
and then whole words as they begin, again.

Biological Warfare

Humankind's capacity for violence --
the way cruelty blinks so quickly
within wronged minds seeking
revenge without a sigh of hesitation

Poison water wells with dead bodies,
catapult plague victims over city walls,
these moments just the beginning
of mankind's ethical fall, what appalling
anger must reside within to reign torture
down upon they who do not sin, those
innocent children and starving laborers

Wine mixed with the blood of lepers
sold to mighty foes, saliva drooled
by rabid dogs washed over traded crops,
threats of poison bullets barely stopped
in time, all of this just beginning
the great violence of humankind

Blankets laced with smallpox
with intent of genocide, discarded
clothes from yellow fever patients
given to Union troops, all coincide
with the inexplicable violence
of the vindictive humankind

VECTOR-BORNE

The birds started dying
crows fell from the sky
like shooting stars
covered in black feathers
an eagle plummeted
straight into the river,
and the zoo's flamingos
stand tall no more

Blood pools in their brains
unknown pathogens taking over
as the last 90's summer closes,
humans begin to die, too --
fire captured their minds
fevers burning so hot
some become paralyzed
while death reaps the others

Small, vicious insects linger
seeking flesh to bite into,
syringe-like mouths drinking,
squirting contaminated saliva
into wounds, into bloodstreams

Birds become vectors
as the mosquitoes drink,
draw up virus-laden blood
into the midgut, fester
mixtures in salivary glands
until a new bird is found,
a new host to brew and transport
infection every year when summer
arrives with bright sun and temptingly
warm nights beside a campfire

Your Garden of Skin and Organs

Your body is a grassy field
where influenza has come to graze

Imagine millions of starving lawn mowers
tearing hungry razors across your mucus,
the protection lining your airway, shredding
through the roots of all that you've grown
within your cherished body, your garden
of skin and organs, the blossoms of resisting
cells, the stems of antibodies -- all destroyed

Look to the stars when it mutates,
when strains reassort genes into new
combinations, deadlier and hungrier,
acceleration of unstoppable change eager
to feed on all the new grassy blades
you have been protecting within the drying
husk of your isolated body, sharp viruses
wielding scythes will come show you
why you can never hide, why there will
always be something new lurking, ready
to bring destruction into your garden,
no matter how many times you regrow.

Underwater Snow

When this is all over,
let's go away, you and I
across the ocean to new
adventures; as we fly over
the vast expanse of sea,
I will tell you of the viruses
floating in the water, how if
you lined each one up
end-to-end, they'd stretch
out 42 million light-years

Our brains unable to make
sense of such numbers,
but I'll trace my fingertips
against your skin, tell you
of bacterial blooms, the way
algae breathes and releases
precious gas, seeding clouds
that help cool the planet

When we arrive we'll go see
those impressive White Cliffs
of Dover, marvel at such splendor
formed from morphing tiny
algae skeletons to chalk,
waiting all those years
below sea level, only to rise

In the grassland we might find
jackdaws and skylarks,
rare buds of spider orchids,
the tell-tale brightness of red
admiral butterflies fluttering
about our heads, and we will

know how all this exquisite life
stemmed from seawater viruses
ripping open a host, sticky
molecules snagging carbon
bits down into the underwater
snowstorm -- how sometimes it takes
great pain and darkness
to seek out even greater beauty